Election Day

For Becky Goodman, who gave me the idea
—M. M.

First Simon Spotlight edition November 2011
First Aladdin Paperbacks edition September 2004

Text copyright © 2004 by Simon & Schuster, Inc.
Illustrations copyright © 2004 by Mike Gordon

SIMON SPOTLIGHT
An imprint of Simon & Schuster Children's Publishing Division
1230 Avenue of the Americas
New York, NY 10020

SIMON SPOTLIGHT, READY-TO-READ, and colophon are registered
trademarks of Simon & Schuster, Inc.

Designed by Sammy Yuen Jr.
The text of this book was set in CentSchbook BT.

Printed in the United States of America
16 18 20 19 17

Library of Congress Cataloging-in-Publication Data
McNamara, Margaret.
Election day / by Margaret McNamara ; illustrated by Mike Gordon.—
1st Aladdin Paperbacks ed.
p. cm.—(Ready-to-read) (Robin Hill School)
Summary: On Becky's first day at a new school, she finds that she has a
chance to run for class president.
ISBN 979-0-689-86425-4 (pbk.)—ISBN 978-0-689-86426-1 (lib. bdg.)
0816 LAK
[1. Elections—Fiction. 2. Schools—Fiction.] I. Gordon, Mike, ill.
II. Title. III. Series.
PZ7.M232518El 2004
[E]—dc22   2003023505

Election Day

Written by Margaret McNamara
Illustrated by Mike Gordon

Ready-to-Read

Simon Spotlight
New York   London   Toronto   Sydney   New Delhi

There was a knock
on Mrs. Connor's
classroom door.

"That is our new student,"
said Mrs. Connor.

"This is Becky,"
said Mrs. Connor.

"Hello, Becky,"
the class said loudly.
"Hello,"
Becky said quietly.

Nia showed Becky where
to sit.

"Can anyone tell Becky
what day it is today?"
asked Mrs. Connor.

"Today is Tuesday,"
said Ayanna.

"Today is election day,"
she said.

"Yes," said Mrs. Connor.
"Today we will vote
for our class
president."

After lunch,
the children gave speeches.
"I promise to get us
a candy machine!"
said Nick.

"Hooray!" said the class.

"I promise no homework!"
said Emma.

"Hooray! Hooray!"
said the class.

"I promise summer vacation
will last for six months!"
said Nia.

"Hooray! Hooray! Hooray!"
said the class.

"Would anyone else like to give a speech?" asked Mrs. Connor.

Becky thought
she could be
a good class president.

But she was new.

She did not have any friends.

She did not have a speech.

"Anyone?"
asked Mrs. Connor.
She was looking
right at Becky.

Becky took a deep breath.
She got up from her chair.

"I cannot promise
candy machines,

or less homework,

or more vacation,"
she said.

"I can only promise
to do my best."
Becky sat down.

No one said a word.
Especially not "Hooray."

"Now," said Mrs. Connor.
"It is time to vote."

The children put their heads
on their desks
and their hands in the air.

Mrs. Connor counted
all the votes.
"Becky is the winner!"
she said.

The new class president
was happy.

"You made a good promise," Hannah said.

"It is a promise I will keep," said Becky.

PALM BEACH COUNTY
LIBRARY SYSTEM
3650 Summit Boulevard
West Palm Beach, FL 33406-4198